DO NOT REMOVE
CARDS FROM POCKET

HENRY CISNEROS

MEXICAN-AMERICAN LEADER

ELIZABETH COONROD MARTINEZ

Hispanic Heritage
The Millbrook Press
Brookfield, Connecticut

Cover photograph courtesy of Max Aguilera-Hellweg

Photographs courtesy of Cisneros Communications: p. 3;
Superstock: pp. 4, 10 (inset), 20; Mrs. Elvira Cisneros: pp.
7, 8, 12, 16; Bettmann: pp. 10, 27, 28; AP/Wide World Photos:
pp. 13, 25; San Antonio *Express-News:* pp. 17 (Steve Krauss),
18 (Jose Barrera), 21 (Trigg Gardner); Gamma-Liaison: p. 22.

Library of Congress Cataloging-in-Publication Data
Martinez, Elizabeth Coonrod, 1954–
Henry Cisneros : Mexican-American leader / by Elizabeth Coonrod
Martinez.
p.   cm.—(Hispanic heritage)
Includes bibliographical references and index.
Summary: A biography of the Mexican-American mayor of San Antonio,
Texas, who became the first Hispanic mayor of a major United States
city in 1981.
ISBN 1-56294-368-5 (lib. bdg.)
1. Cisneros, Henry—Juvenile literature.   2. Mayors—Texas—San
Antonio—Biography—Juvenile literature.   3. Mexican Americans—
Texas—San Antonio—Politics and government—Juvenile literature.
4. San Antonio (Tex.)—Politics and government—Juvenile literature.
[1. Cisneros, Henry.   2. Mayors.   3. Mexican Americans—Biography.]
I. Title.   II. Series.
F394.S2C565   1993
976.4'351063'092—dc20   [B]   92-21384   CIP   AC

Published by The Millbrook Press
2 Old New Milford Road
Brookfield, Connecticut 06804

HENRY CISNEROS

San Antonio is one of the largest cities
in the southwestern United States.

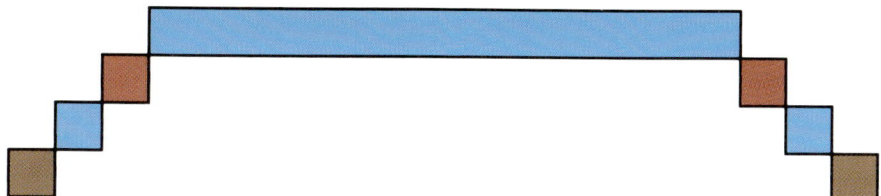

How does a Hispanic become mayor of the tenth-largest city in the United States? Mexican-American Henry Cisneros says he did it through education.

When Henry was a very young boy in San Antonio, Texas, he spent a lot of time at his grandfather's printing press. Henry's grandfather printed newspapers and books. Henry used to listen to the people who brought their papers and books to the press as they talked about what they printed. And he became curious. So he started looking at the things his grandfather printed and taught himself to read them.

Henry's curiosity and interest in reading turned out to have important effects on him. By the time he started school, Henry—whose grandfather came from Mexico—could read both English and Spanish. Henry's reading ability helped him learn so quickly that he skipped a whole year of elementary school. At sixteen, Henry graduated from high school, more than a year before his friends. He went on to earn three college degrees before he was thirty years old.

Henry's early experiences at his grandfather's printing press made him love learning and filled him with ideas about what he wanted to do when he grew up. He decided he wanted to help people. Probably one of the greatest chances to do that in Henry Cisneros's life came in 1981 when he became the very first Mexican-American mayor of his home city, San Antonio, Texas.

Just who is Henry Cisneros, this Hispanic American who rose to the top?

EARLY LIFE AND LEARNING · Henry Gabriel Cisneros was born on June 11, 1947. He was the first child of George and Elvira Cisneros. His father was born in the state of New Mexico, next to Texas. His mother was born in Mexico City, in the country of Mexico, and came to San Antonio with her parents when she was a girl.

In addition to reading, Henry loved to play football and baseball as a boy. Sometimes he played with his brother and two sisters. There were so many other kids in his neighborhood that a complete team for either sport was always easy to find. Kids used to tease Henry about his big ears, but he did not mind much. He also had big dark eyes and a curiosity about people. He liked people. He also liked working by himself. His favorite hobby when he was little was making model airplanes and building big runways for them in his backyard.

Henry in his baseball uniform at Little Flower Elementary School.

Henry's grandfather in one of his rooms of books.

When Henry did not want to be by himself he had many people to visit besides his friends. Many of his uncles and aunts and cousins lived in his neighborhood. He especially liked to visit his grandfather, who had rooms and rooms full of books in his house. His grandfather often marked pages in some books that he wanted Henry to read when he came over.

Henry's parents held long conversations with him and his brother and sisters at the dinner table. His parents would tell him, "Anything you want to be, you can be." Henry dreamed about being a pilot for a while, and asked his dad questions about the armed services, because his dad was a colonel in the U.S. Army.

Although Henry was independent, he listened to what his parents said. He knew their advice was good about many things. His mother taught him to eat healthy foods. She never let Henry or his brother and sisters eat between meals. At dinnertime, the family ate delicious Mexican food made with corn and meat like tamales and enchiladas. Other times they ate spaghetti or a roast with mashed potatoes and gravy.

When Henry became a teenager, he began to write poetry. He was sixteen years old in 1963 when President John F. Kennedy was killed, and he wrote a poem expressing his sadness about it. His poem was considered one of the best poems in all of the San Antonio high schools that year.

Background: Texans fighting for independence from inside the Alamo. The Alamo today flying the Texas flag.

HOME OF THE ALAMO

San Antonio is home to a famous building in Texan history—the Alamo.

In 1718 the Alamo was built by the Spaniards as a Catholic church and a home for priests. When Mexico declared its independence from Spain in 1810, Texas became part of Mexico.

By 1836, however, many people in Texas no longer wanted to belong to Mexico. A small group of these people gathered near the Alamo to fight to free Texas.

The Mexican government sent a large army to stop the group. The Texan group took cover inside the Alamo. On February 23, 1836, the Mexican army warned them to leave, but they would not. Then the Mexican army attacked them. Although the group inside the Alamo was small, they fought the Mexicans. But by 8 A.M. the next day, the Mexicans had won the battle. Only three people in the Alamo survived.

The Texans' fight against Mexico continued. "Remember the Alamo" was its battle cry. On April 21, 1836, the army of Texas under General Sam Houston forced the Mexicans to retreat, and Texas was independent. Later it became part of the United States.

The Alamo, a symbol of Texas's independence, still stands today in San Antonio.

Henry when he graduated from high school at 16.

When Henry finished high school in 1964, he went to Texas A&M University, near the city of Austin, Texas. One year, when a professor scolded Henry because some of his grades were not very good, he studied extra hard and the next year made all A's.

After Henry graduated from college with two kinds of degrees, a bachelor's and a master's, he decided it was time to pursue his goal of helping people. So he began working for the city of San Antonio, in a program that helped poor people. The next year he married Mary Alice Perez, on June 1, 1969. Henry had met Mary Alice in high school. She was very smart and she liked helping people just like Henry did.

LEARNING MORE · Cisneros decided that to achieve his goal he needed to know more about government work. So he and Mary Alice moved to Washington, D.C., where he started working on another degree, a doctorate, at George Washington University. He also got a job with the National League of Cities, an important organization to help people in cities.

Cisneros started his career in the National League of Cities and in 1986 became its president.

Cisneros learned about city problems and how to take care of them. One of the best ways, he discovered, was to hold a political office, such as mayor. That was when he decided he wanted to someday be mayor of his hometown of San Antonio. First, he still had to study more. In 1971 he applied to enter a special program at the White House, under President Richard Nixon. Cisneros and fifteen other persons were the only ones accepted from a group of three thousand people who applied! At the White House, Cisneros learned more about how to work on government problems. It was a busy year but a happy one, especially because the Cisneros's first child, Teresa, was born.

When Cisneros finished the White House program, he decided to go to Harvard University, near Boston, Massachusetts, for one more degree. While he worked hard on his studies at Harvard University, he taught at another college. After two years, he earned a second master's degree. Finally Cisneros felt he was ready to put his education to use.

COMING HOME · In August 1974, the Cisneros family returned to San Antonio. Cisneros started working as a teacher at the University of Texas at San Antonio, and the family moved into a house in the neighborhood where he grew up.

But Cisneros soon discovered San Antonio had problems. Hispanics and non-Hispanics did not get along very well. Non-Hispanic business owners had control of the city government. The Hispanic business owners felt they had no say in how to run the city. Many people wanted the city to grow, but the non-Hispanic people who ran the city were stubborn and would not let things change. Meanwhile, San Antonio's population was growing. Many people did not have jobs. The city streets were not always clean, and prices for water and electricity kept getting higher.

Cisneros decided he could help solve these problems and get Hispanics and non-Hispanics to understand each other. So he decided to run for the office of city councilman, one of the people who helps the mayor.

His family and friends helped him. They talked to people on the phone about him, and mailed out letters and flyers explaining why he would be a good city councilman. Meanwhile, Cisneros talked to people in his neighborhood and many others. He made speeches too, and as people began to hear his ideas many believed he could really help the city, so they voted for him.

In 1975, Henry Cisneros became the youngest city councilman ever elected in San Antonio. It was a happy year all around, for his second daughter, Mercedes, was born that year.

As city council-man, Cisneros liked to be out among people. He had a phone in his car.

As councilman, Cisneros worked hard on the city's problems. People liked his work so much that they elected him councilman two more times, in 1977 and in 1979.

By this time Cisneros had many years of both education and experience. He felt that with more power he could really help people. So he decided he was ready to run for mayor.

BECOMING MAYOR · In 1981, Henry Cisneros saw his chance. He told the people of San Antonio that he would be a better mayor than anybody else—even if he was not white, even though he was a Hispanic-American, even though, at thirty-three, he was not very old yet.

The campaign began. Cisneros spent every day meeting people and sharing their concerns and hopes. On May 1, 1981, both Hispanics and non-Hispanics voted for him. Henry Cisneros became the first-ever Hispanic mayor of a big city in the United States.

As his parents watched, Cisneros took the oath of office of mayor.

Now he had to work harder than ever before. He decided that in order to help the city he had to learn about the problems that people who worked for it faced everyday. He drove around with a policeman to see what kinds of crimes were committed in the city. One day he worked on a garbage truck, picking up garbage all day long. People were shocked.

Finding out the problems of collecting garbage—by doing it.

But they were very impressed. Newspaper people took pictures of him, and the TV stations came out with their cameras too. They asked, "Why are you doing this, Mr. Mayor?" Cisneros said, "So that I can find out what the problems are."

The next day, a newspaper picture appeared of Cisneros using a big electric drill in the street. He was repairing a huge hole that had been in the street for a long time. "If we don't have enough people to do the work to get our streets cleaned up, I'll help do it," he said.

Cisneros changed the way the mayor's job was done. He had a lot of energy and did not want to stay inside his office all day.

This had an effect on the citizens. Pretty soon they said, If the mayor's going to work hard to clean up our city, we'll do it too. Soon many people were cleaning up and repairing the city.

Cisneros did not confine his activity to San Antonio alone. He met with people in other cities and states. Many owned big businesses, and Cisneros convinced them to move their businesses to San Antonio. At first some of the people in San Antonio said, We have to put all the businesses right downtown. However, Mayor Cisneros said, No. We need to put the new businesses in different neighborhoods, so that the people in those neighborhoods who don't have jobs can get jobs. That's how we can help *everybody* in this town.

Left: The San Antonio River runs through the city. While people boat, a mariachi band plays in a park on the banks.

Facing page: Playing football with young San Antonians.

Cisneros also worked hard to help businesses that were already in San Antonio grow. The U.S. Air Force had been a big employer in the city for a long time. To show his support for it, he went up in one of its planes with many newspaper and TV people watching.

Not only did Henry Cisneros work along with the people of San Antonio, he had fun along with them as well. The mayor attended parties and Hispanic celebrations called fiestas. One time he surprised everybody when he got up and sang a song in Spanish with a mariachi band, a traditional Mexican street band.

*In San Antonio murals like this one
depict Mexican history and culture.*

KINDS OF HISPANIC-AMERICANS

In the early 1990s there were 25 million Hispanic-Americans in the United States. More than half of these people were called Mexican-Americans because either they or their relatives came from Mexico.

Henry Cisneros's grandfather on his mother's side, José Rómulo Munguía, was such a person. He was born in Mexico. Both of his parents died when he was 8 years old and he went to work in a printer's shop in Mexico City. When Munguía turned 18, he started his own print shop. In 1926 he moved to San Antonio, Texas, with his family.

There are other Hispanic-Americans whose families have lived in the United States for many generations—even before the United States became the United States. Henry Cisneros's father is one of those people. George Cisneros was born in New Mexico. His family descended from Spanish settlers who arrived two hundred years before the American Revolution. George Cisneros's family were migrants—people who move from place to place in order to work, usually harvesting crops. The Cisneros family moved around picking beets.

Other kinds of Hispanic-Americans come from Puerto Rico and Cuba. Still others come from Latin America. Hispanic-Americans—also known as Latinos—have many different histories and are the fastest growing minority in the United States.

When people got together to play baseball, sometimes the mayor would come and pitch. When they had a running race, he came and ran with them. When it was Independence Day, he made a speech.

Cisneros's popularity was growing. When it came time for re-election and people had to decide if they wanted him to continue as mayor, they said "Yes!" In fact, they said it three times. Henry Cisneros was re-elected in 1983, 1985, and 1987, the same year his son John Paul was born.

HENRY GETS FAMOUS · By now, other people in the country were starting to notice the handsome, friendly, hard-working Hispanic mayor. He was invited to other cities to give speeches and to talk to other government people. They all wanted to find out how he did such a good job.

In 1984, Cisneros was invited to be a guest on the television program called *60 Minutes*. The show's crew brought their TV cameras to San Antonio, and its hosts followed the mayor around. People all over the country learned about Henry on the *60 Minutes* show.

That same year a man named Walter Mondale was running for president of the United States. He saw Mayor Cisneros on the *60 Minutes* show, and came to San Antonio to talk to him. He talked to the mayor about running for vice president of the country with him.

Cisneros, Mercedes, Teresa, and Mary Alice with Walter Mondale.

Cisneros was excited about the chance to be vice president but Mondale did not pick him and did not win the presidential election. So Cisneros continued as mayor. He was still popular. Some people in Texas thought maybe he could be a U.S. senator someday.

But Cisneros decided to just keep working in San Antonio. San Antonio would be a good city, he thought, if everybody were able to do just what he or she wanted to do. He remembered what his parents told him when he was little. So he tried to help people find jobs they wanted by helping them get the education they needed. He made sure that the gas and electricity companies did not charge too much, so the people would have money for school for their children and themselves. He visited officials in the state capital, Austin, and convinced them that San Antonio's university needed to be bigger. That way more people could go there and learn how to do the things they wanted to do. The officials in Austin agreed to provide money for new buildings at the university. Pretty soon, more students attended than ever before.

Mayor Cisneros would often tell people that they needed to make plans. He would say: If you make a plan in your own life, what you want to be when you grow up, and what things you need to study, then you'll get to do what you want to do. If people want to have a good city, the city needs a good plan as well. So Cisneros always made sure San Antonio had a plan.

Henry Cisneros finished being mayor in 1989 and started a business in San Antonio. He became president and owner of that business. He continued making many speeches in cities all around the country, and worked with organizations to help people in San Antonio.

*Making a plan to help Hispanics with
the National Hispanic Agenda.*

Cisneros with Bill Clinton and California senator-elect
Barbara Boxer during the 1992 campaign.

During the 1992 presidential campaign, Cisneros worked very hard to help Bill Clinton. After Clinton won the election, he asked Cisneros to be part of his transition team, a group of people who helped the new president get organized to run the country. Henry Cisneros's education and hard work helped him win the respect of the new president.

President Clinton also valued Cisneros's experience in solving the problems of people in cities. So Clinton appointed him to one of the most important jobs in his administration. In 1993 Henry Cisneros became secretary of the U.S. Department of Housing and Urban Development. As secretary Cisneros became responsible for helping people in cities throughout the United States get the best kind of housing and build the best kind of communities. It was a high honor for this Hispanic-American who started out as a boy in San Antonio, Texas, with a desire to help people and a yearning to read and learn.

IMPORTANT EVENTS IN
THE LIFE OF HENRY CISNEROS

1947   Henry is born on June 11, in San Antonio, Texas.

1964   Henry graduates from Catholic Central High School in San Antonio.

1968–1974   Henry earns bachelor's and master's degrees from A&M University in Texas. He also earns degrees from George Washington and Harvard universities.

1975–1979   Henry, at age twenty-seven, is the youngest city councilman in San Antonio's history.

1981–1989   Henry serves as the first Hispanic mayor in his city's history.

1989   Henry finishes being mayor of the city of San Antonio and starts his own company, Cisneros Communications.

1992   Henry is named a member of President-elect Bill Clinton's transition team.

1993   Henry becomes secretary of the U.S. Department of Housing and Urban Development.

FIND OUT MORE
ABOUT HENRY CISNEROS

Henry Cisneros: Mexican-American Mayor by Maurice Roberts (Chicago: Childrens Press, 1986).

Henry Cisneros: Portrait of a New American by Kemper Diehl and Jan Jarboe (San Antonio: Corona Publishing, 1985).

Señor Alcalde by John Gilles (New York: Dutton, 1988).

ABOUT MEXICAN AMERICANS

Hector Lives in the United States Now: The Story of a Mexican-American Child by Joan Hewett (New York: HarperCollins, 1990).

Portraits of Mexican Americans by Nancy Marquez and Theresa Perez (Carthage, Ill.: Good Apple, 1991).

ABOUT TEXAS

Texans: The Story of Texan Cultures for Young People by Barbara E. Stanush (San Antonio: University of Texas Institute, 1986).

INDEX

Page numbers in *italics* refer to illustrations.